'Twas the Late Night of Christmas

For Nola,
Merry, merry!

Ann Whitford Paul

All best Wishes, Nola

Nancy Hayashi

'Twas the Late Night of Christmas

Ann Whitford Paul
ILLUSTRATIONS BY Nancy Hayashi

eFrog Press

Published by eFrog Press
www.efrogpress.com

ISBN-13: 978-0-9894356-2-8 (Paperback edition)
ISBN-13: 978-0-9894356-1-1 (ebook edition)

Cover and interior design by Lydia D'moch

First edition

To frazzled parents everywhere

—*Nancy and Ann*

'Twas the late night of Christmas,
when all through the house
everyone was exhausted, even the mouse.

The stockings were empty. They drooped on a chair.
I slumped—overwhelmed—deep in despair
for my children were whining, the girl and the boys,
complaining already about all their toys.

"My video game sucks."

"My doll lost her head."

"ENOUGH!"

Father shouted and took them to bed.

I dragged myself up and started to clean
the hurricane mess, the worst that I'd seen—

red and green papers smushed in a mound;
cards, boxes, and ribbons tossed all around;
dirty dishes and glasses, pots and pans, too.

"AGGHHHHHHHH!"

I screamed like a wicked-witch shrew.

Out on the lawn there arose such a clatter,
I rushed to the door to see what was the matter.

Cloaks of thick snow covered the ground.
The trees stood like kings, icicle crowned.

When what to my wondering eyes should appear,
but a miniature sleigh led by tiny reindeer,
with a little old driver, white-haired and quick,
I knew right away it was . . .

. . . Mrs. Saint Nick.

She parked in our yard, clambered out of the sled,
and greeted me with a slight bow of her head.

Then she rushed in the house
and poured me sweet tea.

"Your job now is nothing.
Just sit and watch me."
She surveyed all the clutter.
Like an angry clerk,
she rolled up her sleeves
and went right to work.

She scrubbed all the pans. She washed every plate.
In the blink of an eye, she packed up a crate
with the boxes and bags.

She grunted and groaned
and dusted and swept 'til everything shone.

I walked her back out to her sled in the yard,
and gave her a hug, heartfelt and hard.

I heard her complain ere she drove out of sight,
"My husband has fun on Christmas Eve night,

BUT . . .

. . . I'm forced to follow and set things back *right*."

ANN WHITFORD PAUL is crazy for Christmas. Each December she decks her house with handmade decorations—patchwork quilts, ribbon and needlepoint pillows, tablecloths, Santa toys and pictures of snowmen, angels, and gingerbread men. Putting everything out is a joy, but after the holiday is over, she'd love Mrs. Saint Nick to come pack it away so she can return to writing. She lives in Los Angeles and has published nineteen books for children and adults.

For more information, visit AnnWhitfordPaul.net.

NANCY HAYASHI sometimes longs for the snowy winters of her hometown in Ohio. A favorite Christmas memory is rescuing her kitten from the top of the tree, where it was hanging on to the angel. The angel's wings were never the same after that. Now she lives in Los Angeles and illustrates picture books.

Mrs. Saint Nick shares tips to put the joy back in Christmas at MrsSaintNick.wordpress.com.

CPSIA information can be obtained
at www.ICGtesting.com
Printed in the USA
LVIC05n0838081113
360483LV00001B/1